HIDE-AND-SEEK

A SHORT STORY

INCLUDED IN 'YOUR MOTHER'S NIGHTMARES', A
COLLECTION OF SIX TROUBLING TALES

ANITHA KRISHNAN

DREAM PEDLAR BOOKS

For Dhruv,
the greatest miracle in my life.
How can you ever disappear from sight, when I carry you in my
heart at all times? Thank you for giving me the experience of a love
so unparalleled, so sublime, my very soul is now imbued with it.

ABOUT THIS BOOK

Hide-and-Seek

Every child's favourite game. One mother's worst nightmare.

In a seemingly endless game of hide-and-seek, a mother looks for her child in all his favourite hiding spots. But he has hidden himself so well she's unable to find him.

Then she comes up with the perfect bait to coax him out. His favourite toys!

Will they entice him to reveal himself? Or has she been playing the wrong game all along?

Hide-and-Seek secured an Honourable Mention in the Spring/Summer 2021 issue of Allegory Magazine, Volume 39/66.

BEFORE WE BEGIN

Dear Reader,

Motherhood, or even parenting in general, is one of those life experiences that are almost universal yet remarkably unique to each one of us.

Everyone's parenting journey is vastly different. What works for one parent/family may simply not work for another.

My own journey has been a mix of unimaginable joys and unbelievable anxieties and everything else in between these two extremes.

During those dark moments, I turned to writing as a salve. I couldn't bring myself to speak aloud the fears I had for my child. Already wracked with anxiety and a deep sense of wrongness for even having those fears in the first place, I was terrified that putting them in written or spoken form—by journalling or talking about them to someone—might just make them come true.

Instead, I couched them in the guise of speculative fiction to render them more palatable, more surmountable, and as a reminder that in those moments my fears were exactly that—fiction!

It's for this very reason that I crafted the short story collection, *Your Mother's Nightmares*, a few months ago. *Hide-and-Seek* is a short story from that six-tale collection.

If you're a parent, my hope is that in these pages, you too will find the words for the darkness you already know so intimately and grapple with every single day, and emerge into the light on the other side, feeling seen and sane and safe in the knowledge that you are doing the best you can and that is more than enough.

~ *Anitha Krishnan*
Burlington, Ontario,
Monday, 24 June 2024

HIDE-AND-SEEK

1

You've become terrific at playing hide-and-seek.

There was a time, not too long ago, when you were only too eager to give yourself away. A not-so-muffled giggle. A deliberately conspicuous thump. A noisy swish of fabric.

And when all else failed, I only had to ask, "Where are you?", and the shape of you would burst into view. Like a dolphin leaping, breaking the surface of the ocean, you'd plunge into the void of your absence, shouting, "Here!", and career into my arms.

"Where are you?" I holler now. My voice is hoarse from all the times I've called out to you since morning.

You remain quiet and hidden, as if you have finally understood the rules of the game and discovered a compulsive urge to abide by them.

2

—————

*S*ix months before you were born, I started to read aloud to you every day, determined to pass on my love of words to you. *Possum Magic* and a slew of other books by Mem Fox. *Room On The Broom* by Julia Donaldson.

When you were ten months old, you decided that books were for ripping pages from. That was when I learnt about board books and the importance of storing newspapers and pamphlets instead of tossing them into the bin unread.

When you were two years old, you paused me in the middle of a reading of a *Thomas the Tank Engine* story and asked, "How can we go inside this book?"

I stared at you for a few moments, awed by the simple sincerity on your face. And while you waited patiently for a reply, I swallowed all the words that threatened to tumble out of my mouth, for none was worthy of constituting a response to your innocence.

"How can we go inside this book?" you asked again, misconstruing my silence for inattention. "We need to find a way," you insisted, devouring the images of the shiny red and bright blue and gleaming green trains puffing busily around the island of Sodor.

"Well," I said, "take a good look at the pictures. Then close your eyes and you'll see all the trains in your mind."

Lame, I know. It didn't fool you either.

I look for you now in your reading nook under the bottom shelf of your closet.

A blue plush mat covers most of the floor and a small beige pillow with the image of an orange fox on its cover rests on it. A teddy rests against the pillow and a reading lamp looms over it.

All your picture books lie scattered in this space, some open to well-thumbed pages. I resist the urge to snap them shut and stack them in a neat pile. What if you've indeed found a way to slip inside any of them and are still working your way out?

3

———

When you were not really two anymore but also not yet three, and I resolutely refrained from referring to you as an almost-three-year-old for I didn't want time to hurtle any faster than it already was, you asked me what monsters and ghosts were.

Had we just read *The Monster Under The Shed*, a Thomas the Tank Engine tale? Or was it Brigitte Weninger's *Davy, Help! It's a Ghost!*

I recall neither which book it was nor my answer, which surely must have been inept, for it didn't take you long to figure out that whatever or whoever they were, real or imagined, monsters and ghosts were something to be terrified of.

I look for you under my bed, a place you believed would never be invaded by anything petrifying. Dust bunnies and cobwebs shiver like drifting mist under my laborious breath.

Even through their haze, I can see your little yellow excavator is gone. A-ha! So you did sneak in here, after all.

I hurry downstairs and rummage in your toybox. A sleek, red convertible catches my eye. I grab it and run back up and slip it like an offering under my bed.

4

———

When you were three, you asked me about God. Actually, no. You asked me why the church bells rang. Despite my convent school education, I didn't know much about churches, and I told you so. "Why?" you asked.

Later that evening, after you had fallen fast asleep, I opened the boxes in the basement until I found the one I was looking for. The next morning, you noticed the tiny altar I had set up in a corner of the kitchen.

The Gods of my childhood are exotic. One has the face and tail of a monkey. Another has the head of an elephant.

One has indigo skin and a peacock feather in his crown. "Blue person," you observed.

Another wears a cobra as a necklace.

Nestled in the congregation of idols and framed images on the altar was a standing crucifix, an acquisition from my convent school days.

I told you the names of all those Gods and whatever little of their stories I knew. And I also told you those were merely stories. People like to make up stories about everything and everyone unfamiliar to them.

God is as real as *Thomas the Tank Engine* could ever be, I explained, pleased with my deployment of simile.

"Like monsters and ghosts," you chimed in.

5

———

When you were four, you asked me about death. Yet again, I talked to you about the myriad stories people make up about death and all that comes beyond it.

But this time, with much more conviction than I had been able to muster in our discussions about monsters and ghosts and Gods, I said to you, "No one really knows what happens when we die. Anyone who tells you otherwise is lying."

"But we can imagine?" you suggested and asked at the same time.

"Sure. Maybe we become stars?"

"Maybe we become trees?"

"Maybe our bodies become part of the earth and help other things grow." And I wondered if the residual ashes of cremated bodies could help sustain new life too.

After a few days of silence on the topic, you declared, "I know what happens after we die, Mumma."

You were trying to put on your shoes by yourself and I was

sitting on the floor beside you, hands clasped together, trying hard to resist the uncontrollable urge to help you.

"What happens?" I asked, doubling my efforts at maintaining a façade of patience and calm.

"We come back again," you said.

"That could very well be," I said, determined to accept your hypothesis but also not completely eliminate its inherent uncertainty.

"That is how it is, Mumma," you insisted. "I know. We come back as another person. We always come back."

And I had to concede you may have somehow coaxed a secret from the very belly of this Universe.

6

The creek where it happened is the last place I search, convinced you wouldn't come back to the very spot where we had inadvertently begun our unending game of hide-and-seek, your turn to hide and mine to seek, and you had simply vanished. I didn't expect to find you here but now that you are nowhere in sight, I am sorely disappointed.

Gloomy clouds have gathered on the horizon and they now soar towards me. The distant rumble of thunder rolls across the sky like a landslide.

Everyone thinks lightning doesn't strike the same place twice, but it does. It did the last time we were here, in this very place where I now lie spread-eagled like an X marking the spot where the only treasure I ever had was last seen alive and has since vanished.

A part of me wishes to hang around and see if lightning will strike here a third time now, so I will never need to think or do anything ever again because I am so tired, I am so, so tired, but another part of me insists I must run back home before the storm arrives because I still haven't found you and our game is not over yet.

7

Are ghosts for real?
Does God exist?
What happens to us when we die?
Funny how I am the one with all the questions and you are the one with all the answers now.

8

Sleep eludes me all night. In the brief flashes of illumination that lightning brings, I keep my eyes peeled for you. But no shadows move, no unexplained silhouettes appear.

When the storm passes at the break of dawn, I will myself off the bed and peek under.

Et voila! The red convertible has disappeared!

Hope propels me down the stairs and I throw open your toybox, wondering if I should place your next offering somewhere more visible to me, so I can watch you come in to fetch it.

But there they are. Atop the little jumble of vehicles you gleaned endless delight from, lie your yellow excavator and red convertible. Did you put them back last night? Or have they been lying here since the last time you and I cleaned up and put away your toys before bedtime?

I fall down, my legs having abruptly forgotten their function to hold me up. My heart aches so much I think it will explode and I want it to. I want it to stop beating, stop trying so hard to keep me alive.

I turn to one side and curl into a foetal position, the way you were cocooned in my womb all those months when I came up with false pretexts to schedule ultrasound appointments just so I could see you even when you were hidden inside of me.

At first, you were a mere flash of blinking light, which the technician declared was your beating heart. Months later, your spine unfurled like a railway track.

At every visit, your heartbeat was like the gallop of a racehorse, as if somehow even back then, even before you were born, you knew you'd zip through this lifetime at the speed of lightning.

Sleep finally arrives as an accomplice to exhaustion.

As I give in, yearning to be completely deprived of all thought and sensation, something presses into the small of my back and reminds me of the way your knees would push into me in the middle of the night as you'd try to curl yourself into a ball and snuggle up to me at the same time.

Something else rakes my hair gently like an extraordinarily wide-toothed comb, and I do what I've always done whenever your fingers have sought out a comforter.

I lift my head and without turning back, I untie my ponytail and bunch it back into a bun I pile atop my head. The familiar tug resumes as something prods and holds on to my bun and after a few moments, whatever it is, finally rests, unstirring, in peace, warm and gentle, beside me.

9

"Are you OK?" This was the one question you never liked me asking you.

The last time you told me off for hurling this question your way was when we had gone to pay our neighbour, two doors down, a brief visit, and her dog, Daisy, burst across their threshold and barrelled into your chest as if she were meeting a long lost lover.

You stood patiently as Daisy sniffed and licked and nudged you, perhaps wishing her paws would somehow morph into arms she could wrap around you. You were only a child's head taller than she was.

Our neighbour pulled Daisy back and I bent to ask you, "Are you OK?" You deigned to answer that question with only a slight nod.

When we returned home, you admonished me, "If I don't say anything, it means I am OK."

10

I won't ask if it is you.

I won't ask if you are OK.

To give in to the urge to verify is to admit doubt. To believe without demanding any more evidence is to have faith.

If I don't seek you anymore, perhaps you will no longer feel the need to hide.

Ready for more fantasy short stories on the motherhood experience? Check out the collection, Your Mother's Nightmares: Six Troubling Tales, which includes five more twisted tales on the motherhood experience.

When you buy the collection directly from my store, please treat yourself to a 40% discount using the code YMN40.

Please note the code YMN40 is valid only for the short story collection — Your Mother's Nightmares: Six Troubling Tales — in ebook format when purchased directly from my PayHip store, Dream Pedlar Books.
Go to https://payhip.com/b/SfQvj to redeem your code!

ENJOYED HIDE-AND-SEEK?

Thank you for reading *Hide-and-Seek*!

If you loved the story, I hope you will consider writing a short review—even a simple line or two—on the site where you bought the book.

Publishing is still driven by word of mouth, and when you leave a review it helps other readers decide this is a story worth reading. Thank you for your help in spreading the word.

You can also sign up to my monthly newsletter for updates on new book releases as well as heartfelt reflections on writing, reading, parenting and living the creative life.

Monthly Missives from The Dream Pedlar
https://thedreampedlar.com/newsletter

AUTHOR'S NOTE

Dear Reader,

Of the six speculative fiction tales on motherhood in the collection, *Your Mother's Nightmares*, if I had to choose one favourite story, *Hide-and-Seek* would be it.

Every dialogue in this tale is one I've had with D in real life. Every single one of them.

From wondering how we can get inside a book, inside a story, to referring to a small idol of Krishna as a blue person, to declaring that we come back after we die … all these conversations happened in real life.

Once we turned to the last page of a picture book—it didn't have any text in it—and D was waiting for me to read. I realized then that he thought I was reading the story from the pictures. This was long before he fell into the words of letters and alphabets, the world of literacy.

I used to maintain a Notes app in which I diligently recorded some of the amazingly imaginative things D used to say in his younger days. I compiled them in a blog post on D's fifth birthday—titled *The Poetry of Growing Older*—when it became evident that this innocent part of himself was fast slipping away.

I share some of them here.

~

D: I feel like the clouds are going to fall.
Me: What will happen then?
D: We will carry them on our heads.

~

D (noticing a hole in the knee of his pyjama one morning): Why is there a hole in my pyjama?
Me: It is worn out, sweetie.
D: Do T-shirts get worn out?
Me: Yes.
D: Do people get worn out?

~

D (at the park on a very windy spring morning): Stop this windy thing, Mumma.

~

D, looks at himself in the mirror and yells, "Mumma, I found myself!"

~

D (at bedtime): Mumma, keep hugging me till tomorrow morning.

~

You can read many more of these delightful utterances on my blog.

https://thedreampedlar.com/the-poetry-of-growing-older/

~

Thank you for reading this far. I'd love to stay in touch with you. And I hope you'd like to stay connected with me too.

I send out a monthly newsletter on the last Sunday of every month filled with heartfelt musings on the joys of writing, reading and living the creative life. Subscription is free.

You will be the first to hear of my forthcoming works. I also include updates on my writing life, book recommendations, free short fiction, and occasional surprises.

Thank you for staying with me this far. If you choose to accompany me further on this journey, I promise you a magical ride.

Climb aboard at https://thedreampedlar.com/newsletter!

~ Anitha Krishnan
Burlington, Ontario
Monday, 24 June 2024

MORE BOOKS BY ANITHA KRISHNAN

https://thedreampedlar.com/books/

Dying Wishes

Finalist, 2023 Rakuten Kobo Emerging Writer Prize in Speculative Fiction

A contemporary fantasy novel weaving Hindu mythology and South Indian folklore into a quest for belonging across different worlds — the World of Mortals and the World of Gods, India and Canada, the past and the present, the world outside and the one within.

Erased from Existence

A paranormal mystery in which a fifteen-year-old is erased from the memories and perception of everyone. Trapped in oblivion, she will have to unearth and reveal long-buried family secrets to escape.

The Land of No Reflection

A fantasy tale of two sightless young women on the run from their homeland, having committed the unpardonable crime of seeing.

A Benevolent Goddess

A story of a goddess who is punished for her desire to help human beings but is unable to find salvation by any other means.

In Search of Leo

A fantasy tale exploring the gamut of emotions that loss and grief can stir.

The Mind Meddler

A short fantasy story on the games The Mind Meddler plays by sneaking thoughts into people's minds, until he meets the one person who can resist his unkind mischief.

Mrs. D'Souza's Dispute With God

A fantasy short story in which a school teacher, Mrs. D'Souza, dies unexpectedly and sets out in search of God to demand answers to her burning questions on life and death.

Hello, Dreamer! Poems & Dreams

An eclectic collection of 100 short poems encompassing musings on the universe and its mysteries, nature and human life, my secret longings and fears, love and heartbreak, the sun and the moon, the stars and the seas, light and shadow, and joy and nostalgia.

ABOUT THE AUTHOR

Anitha Krishnan is a speculative fiction author and an award-winning poet. Her fantasy novel, *Dying Wishes*, was a finalist for the 2023 Rakuten Kobo Emerging Writer Prize in the Speculative Fiction category.

She has lived in and left pieces of her heart in many places across the world including Singapore, Australia, Canada, and most of all in her beloved birthplace, India. She presently lives in Burlington, Ontario with her husband and their cherished child.

Find more books and her blog on the writing life at
https://thedreampedlar.com.

Sign up to her monthly newsletter at
https://thedreampedlar.com/newsletter
to receive heartfelt musings, exclusive updates, book recommendations, free fiction, and more!